The Refugees' Daughter

Takuji Ichikawa

An author who ignores traditional boundaries, and is impossible to pigeonhole. One whose positive and fantastical narratives touch the soul through storytelling that not only 'transforms and heals', but also sells in the millions.

Ichikawa, one of Japan's most creative authors with a completely unique perspective – even by Japanese standards – dreamt of becoming an author at primary school. He firmly believes in the transformative power of imagination; that dreams can come true, and that we can change the world we live in for the better.

After initially publishing stories on the Internet, his second novel *Be With You* became a blockbuster, selling more than a million copies in Japan, putting Ichikawa on the Japanese literary map.

The publication of *Be With You*, in fact, triggered its very own cycle of creativity by sparking the imagination of others, leading to the creation of a film and two international remakes, a television drama, and a manga.

Ichikawa's works, which often depict love and loss, continue to resonate and be adapted for film both in Japan and further afield, and he continues to consistently demonstrate that literature should have no borders.

Translator: Emily Balistrieri

Emily Balistrieri is an American translator based in Tokyo. Published translations include Tomihiko Morimi's *The Night is Short, Walk on Girl*; Ko Hiratori's *JK Haru is a Sex Worker in Another World*; Carlo Zen's *The Saga of Tanya the Evil*, and Kugane Maruyama's *Overlord*.

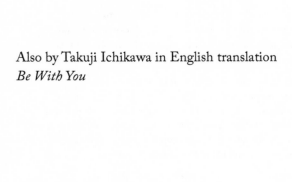

Also by Takuji Ichikawa in English translation
Be With You

A full publication list of all of Ichikawa's work is available from
www.redcircleauthors.com

The Refugees' Daughter

Takuji Ichikawa

Translated from the Japanese by
Emily Balistrieri

Red Circle

Published by Red Circle Authors Limited
First edition 2019
1 3 5 7 9 10 8 6 4 2

Red Circle Authors Limited
Third Floor, 24 Chiswell Street,
London EC1Y 4YX

Red Circle
www.redcircleauthors.com

Takuji Ichikawa has asserted his right under the Copyright, Designs
and Patents Act 1988 to be identified as the author of this work.

Design by Aiko Ishida, typesetting by Danny Lyle
Set in Adobe Caslon Pro

ISBN: 978-1-912864-08-9

A catalogue record of this book is available from the British Library.

To all the important women who continue to make a difference, especially my mother and wife who taught me the meaning of love

The Refugees' Daughter

'Tomorrow, I'm going through the gate.

Where it leads, no one can say for sure. Of course they can't. Not a single person who has gone through has ever come back. But some people have heard their *broadcasts*. Refugees trade rumours in low voices.

A *broadcast* is, I guess, similar to some sort of psychic reaction. The voices talk to us as if they're coming in over a badly-tuned radio. It's usually sensitive children who can hear the *broadcasts*, and these types of special powers appear to be some kind of end-of-times development. That repeating pattern – that *when a species falls into crisis, another branch of it appears* – is apparently true.

Actually, I have that power a little bit, and I've heard Yusuke's voice a few times. It always sounds so far away and foggy, though – more like an echo of an emotion than a voice.

But the echo beckons. Maybe I'm crazy, but I can't help but think he's calling out to me. So I've been wanting to go forever – to escape this world full of hatred and violence and go where he's waiting for me.

I feel that betting everything on love when you're not sure if you'll even be alive tomorrow is absolutely the right choice for a 16-year-old girl. I'd rather live my life for love, not war.

According to the *broadcasts*, where they are is a snow-white world. *What* is white, I don't know. The information is like a lingering scent, never stable.

They say it's very quiet there. In this world, gunshots and explosions thunder non-stop, and shouts and screams are the background noise of daily life. If that all disappeared instantly, anybody would go insane. We're so used to the madness that we're starting to forget what a calm life is like.

In any case, the other side of the gate is supposedly much safer than here. The *broadcasts* guarantee it – 'It's peaceful here'.

But they say things that worry me, too.

'There's something here…' The voice had sounded anxious and on guard. 'I sense some kind of presence…' We don't know if it's friend or foe. It could be The Builders.

The Builders are the ones who made the gate and the white world on the other side. At least that's what we started calling them at some point. There are all sorts of competing theories for who The Builders really are: aliens, people from the future, the remnants of an ancient civilisation. Some people even say they're gods.

Well, anyhow, no matter who made the gate and the white world, they exist for real, and they're waiting for us to come. Is this the hand of benevolent salvation or a villainous trap? Even if intentions are good, can we survive there? Food and water are especially important. Even if there's no war there, without water, we'll die in a matter of days. (The gate is said to disappear after roughly 48 hours, so if that's true we won't be able to come back.) The *broadcasts* just aren't clear on that point, so in the end we have to risk our lives on this one-way ticket without knowing. That's probably why there are so few people who go through.

Still, we're going. We'll pass through the gate. That's what my family decided. We all agree. This resolve won't waver.'

Supposedly, the gate first opened two years ago. Back then, most of the world was in a horrible state, and lots of people believed the end – for this world – was probably nigh.

'How did it all start?' I always wonder. Up until just a few years ago, all I had to worry about was my marks at school and the spots I was starting to get. Of course, we heard an unbearable amount of bad news: the one-to-a-billion wealth disparity. How global warming had crossed the point of no return. Scenes of forests and farmland turned to deserts and people fighting for food and water in countries suffering drought seemed to be on TV every day.

But back then it was just a fire on another shore. We were well enough off and had everything we needed – to the point that we even complained about it, saying, 'If I eat that I'll get fat' or 'Those clothes are already out of style'. (My father says that's called 'repressive desublimination'.)

'Maybe the end of the century will be awful, but during my lifetime things'll be fine.' Turns out that was actually a naive hope. There was no 'other shore'. Everything was happening on this shore – we just didn't see it. Like blindfolded livestock in a truck, we had no idea where we were heading. Maybe the main reason the world ended up as it did was that ignorance and apathy.

It had been early when we left the refugee camp, but now the sun was already down. Afraid of being spotted by government troops or the guerillas, we kept off paved roads as much as possible, instead choosing to walk farm roads or wilderness paths that looked deserted. It was 30 more kilometres to the gate.

Everyone was exhausted. 'Everyone' was me and my family – my mother, my father and my little brother, Takuya – plus Mr Akai, his wife and their daughter, Aoi.

Up ahead we could see the dark silhouette of an embankment. It drew a gentle curve as it continued all the way to a big forest. Suddenly, my father stopped in his tracks. 'Someone's there!'

A wave of anxiety swept through the group. 'Is it government soldiers?' asked Mr Akai.

'No, doesn't seem to be. There's a very large number of them walking along the embankment.'

When I strained my eyes, I was eventually able to see them, too. Dark figures walked on the dirt path at the bottom of the embankment like a string of prayer beads. They were in small clusters heading north.

'They appear to be fellow travelers,' my father said. 'We must have bumped into the path of refugees heading north.'

'Should we join them? Maybe we can get some information.'

'Let's do that.'

We headed for the embankment.

Once we approached, we saw that they were indeed refugees. All of their faces were haggard. They wore backpacks like us and carried large bags. An old man with a cane, an old woman with a shawl over her head, a husband tugging the hand of his pregnant wife – they were all people who had escaped this far, hoping to put even the slightest distance between them and the conflict. We joined the flow.

My father spoke to the family walking next to us. They were a mother, a father and four children. 'Is this route safe?'

The father looked up at us. His jaw was covered in stubble. 'Yes,' he nodded with a tired look on his face. 'At least, that's what we've heard. There's no guarantee, but…'

'How far are you going?'

He said the name of a town. 'We'll go to the coast and catch a boat. We heard there are pirates in the channel, but our plan is to take a big detour.'

My father took out a map and checked the location of the town with his pocket torch. 'Oh, here. Our destination is further inland, so we'll end up parting ways in about ten kilometres…'

When my father pointed at the map with his finger, the man seemed somewhat surprised. 'Why would you go there? Isn't it dangerous? The area just up ahead is under anti-government guerilla control.'

'Yes, that's exactly where we're heading.'

'But that's so reckless!' He looked at us in shock. 'As I just said, the route through the channel can no longer be considered safe. And rumour has it there are Complex mercs up in the northern part of the occupied territory. Almost all the refugees have abandoned that route.'

My father thought for a moment and then cautiously started speaking again. 'Actually… we're not heading for the channel. Our destination is much closer than that… A different shelter.'

The pair looked at each other for a few moments.

'You mean…' the man said after thinking for a little while. 'One of you received the info…?'

'My daughter,' my father said.

The man looked at me and asked: 'When was it?'

'Yesterday around midday,' I answered.

'It's reliable? Not a rumour you heard from someone?'

'It's reliable. I received the announcement myself.'

He fell silent. After surveying our group he looked back at me. 'So it really exists, huh…? It wasn't just a story…'

'That's right,' my father nodded. 'What do you think? Would you like to come with us? Your whole family.'

The man immediately shook his head. 'No, we can't. But…' He thought in silence for a moment. Then he shook his head again. 'No, we really can't. We have to try crossing the sea first. That's why we walked all this way…'

'Yes, that makes sense,' my father said. 'That decision takes a lot of courage, too.'

Nothing else was said about the gate. He warned us not to tell too many people. 'There might be government-army spies, you know? Best to be careful...'

Then the two fathers told each other about their journeys so far. They both seemed used to it. It was the type of information that refugees regularly exchanged when they met.

'How's the food and water situation?' my father asked, and the other man shrugged.

'Ah, it's just awful. Even if you hear rumours of rations and rush over, there are too many people, so you can't really get anything. I once lined up half a day for a single roll. We saw a lot of orphans. They're desperate. They could die tomorrow of hunger if they don't get hold of any rations today. I've given up my spot in the queue before – it's impossible not to...'

He silently shook his head, with sadness on his face. 'We're fine. We have savings, so if we cut into them, we can buy food on the black market. But those children...' He choked up suddenly and went quiet after that.

My father nodded without saying anything. All the refugees felt the same way.

Long years of drought and flooding had dealt a catastrophic blow to the world's agriculture. There was almost no food (or drinkable water, or fuel). Yet a handful of people were trying to monopolise supplies. The reason anti-government soldiers raided warehouses was to take the food and fuel stockpiled by that handful of people and distribute it to the masses who were starving. The reason they were called 'anti-government forces' was that the government were merely the henchmen of that handful of people. The giant corporations covering the planet and their owners, the politicians and soldiers working to protect the rights of those corporations, and the media that handles their PR – all together we call them The Complex. Like a chimera, it's a terrifying monster created with a mix of many different genes. These people are greedy and aggressive; they tend to be arrogant and act as if they own the planet. They're obese vampires who leech away people's happiness. To sustain just one of them, a billion people end up in a joyless, anaemic-like state.

'During childhood, at least, people deserve unconditional happiness...' the man murmured quite a while later. 'If we could have guaranteed that, the world wouldn't have ended up like this... We adults are to blame...'

Even after nine at night, we were still walking. Apparently just a little way further was a temple the refugees used as a rest stop. Much of it had collapsed in the previous year's artillery battle, but it was still sufficient to stay out of the nighttime dew. We were planning on sleeping a bit there, as well.

For a while we had been hearing the sound of far-off bombardments. We saw military helicopters, too, as they flew eastwards across the sky. Were people killing each other again? A man who had climbed onto the embankment shouted that he could see lights from tracers. I grabbed Aoi's hand and tried going up.

Far to the east, much closer to the coast, a town was burning. Low-hanging clouds reflecting the flames were tinted the colour of blood. If I squinted, I could see the tracer lights. And I could hear the dull *boom-boom* of bursting shells. Looking around, I noticed that quite a few refugees had climbed up the embankment to take in the view. The refugees illuminated in the starlight seemed like ancient ghosts that only appeared at night.

I often used to watch the nighttime displays of war like this with Yusuke. We would climb up to the roof of a building, half in ruins, near the shelter, our bodies tinted red in the distant flames.

As we watched one night, a bomber glided over and laid a number of big fiery eggs that fell to the ground. The tracer lights drew broken arches through the night sky.

'It reminds me of being in the city,' Yusuke had said. 'It's like a video on replay. Or is this a dream?'

'Maybe,' I said. 'It could be a never-ending nightmare.'

'In that case, the gate is a portal to awakening.'

'What kind of world will be waiting for us when our eyes open?'

'A world without hatred or war,' he said, kissing my hair. 'I'm sure we'll be able to live there in peace.'

I put a hand to my heart and said, 'So that's what this tells you?'

'Yup,' Yusuke laughed softly. 'It's the instinct of monkeys who hate war, a special form of radar only refugees have.'

That was only less than a year ago, but for some reason it feels as if it was a very long time ago. I missed him so much, it was almost unbearable. *'Yusuke, where are you now?'*

We reached the temple a little before ten.

It was an old temple in a rural village. When we entered the building, there were ten groups already inside. Several people gathered together, forming islands. They glowed hazily in their lamplights.

I lay down right away and closed my eyes. Next to me my father and the couple we met on the embankment were talking about something in low voices. I half-listened to them as I dozed.

'…So you *are* Mr Ikawa? I thought I had seen you somewhere before… Darling, he's a novelist…'

'Oh, wow. It's an honour to meet you…'

'No, no, the pleasure's mine.'

'Quite a few people mentioned *The Kindness Circuit* on this trip. There are a lot of people reading it and comparing it to our reality…'

'I've heard similar things…'

'Some even consider it a book of prophecy…'

'A book of prophecy?'

'Yes. They think there must be some reason the government banned *The Kindness Circuit*…'

'Thanks to that ban, I've been blacklisted. Both the government soldiers and anti-government guerillas are after me. There's nowhere left to run…'

'Oh, so that's why you're heading for the gate?'

'That's one reason. Although it's not just that…'

'…I like that one scene… Where the boy leader says that December 25th is the day that total kindness in the world peaks. And he talks about the Christmas truce that took place on The Western Front. How it all started with a song called 'Silent Night'…'

'Yes, that's right. You have a good memory.'

'Wouldn't it be great if that happened now? If a single song could calm the storm of hate and slaughter whipping through this world…?'

'…I feel the same way…'

'…I'm sure your novel is a prophecy… I want to believe it is. Words possess the power to change reality. People we know as founders of religions have been changing the world like that, with words, for thousands of years…'

The next day we got up at four and set out. The other refugees were all still asleep. We decided to leave without saying anything. The sky was pitch black, and an astonishing number of stars were twinkling in it. Sticking close together, we left the temple.

We took a country road between low mountains. Every house we saw was dilapidated, and there was absolutely no indication of people. The only sounds were the discontented cries of crows.

As we were entering the town we'd been aiming for, the sky was finally starting to lighten in the east. There was still some time left before dawn.

It was a total ghost town. All the shops, cafes, and bars were abandoned. It felt like the set of a horror film.

'The map seems to be right,' my father said. 'There should be a factory down this street. That's where we're heading.'

'The gate is inside the factory?' asked Mr Akai.

My father nodded yes. 'According to the map, the gate should be near the centre of the factory.'

'What level of discrepancy can we expect?'

'Twenty or thirty metres at most. We should be able to tell when we're close.'

As my father had said, the road took us to the factory's back entrance. There were about 50 more metres to the entrance. It was chained up.

'We're almost there,' Takuya said happily. 'We won't have to walk anymore…'

Just then we heard the distant sound of gunfire. Everyone turned around, startled.

'Where are they?!' my father shouted.

'Back in the direction we came from,' Mr Akai said, keeping his voice low.

More shots. It sounded like popcorn cooking in a frying pan. They were automatic rifles, and we could hear other guns firing back.

'Who's shooting?' I asked, and my father shook his head.

'I don't know. Government troops and anti-government guerillas…? Or maybe Complex mercenaries?'

'Mercenaries…'

This country had been split into special districts – domains of capitalists from the great powers. After the droughts and flooding had continued for a few years, people called 'farmland buyers' began snapping up the land at higher latitudes, which had suffered comparably less damage, at a furious pace. Apparently, if the land in their own country was no good, they felt they could just take some from somewhere else. They didn't just appropriate the land, but its water as well. Water had become a valuable commodity.

The government soldiers weren't the only ones anxious to find the gate – the capitalists were too. Naturally, their aim was to seize whatever resources might be waiting in the new world. They apparently wanted to beat everyone there and take everything for themselves. It felt similar to colonisation in the Age of Discovery. I could practically hear the slogan, *Conquer the New World!*

'Did they follow us?' asked Mr Akai.

'Maybe… Anyway, let's hurry. This is our chance – while they're fighting.'

We all set off running for the rear entrance. I took Takuya's hand. 'Hang in there! We've almost made it!'

Takuya nodded, his round forehead slicing through the wind.

Mr Akai reached the entrance first. He rattled the chains to check how strong they were. 'It's no good!' he yelled. 'These are pretty sturdy! We'll have to climb.'

'Go on ahead!' my father shouted in a booming voice as he ran.

Mr Akai nodded and got right to it. He must be very athletic because he was over the fence in the blink of an eye. Next the adults helped the three children over. Then the mothers came. My father helped both of them, his hands steadying their hips. 'Hurry! There's no time!'

The gunshots came closer. They were clearly heading this way. The sounds came from a couple of different directions now, as if the soldiers had split up.

'You can do it! Just a little further!'

First Aoi's mother came over, and mine landed shortly after. The only one left was my father.

The gunfire didn't stop. I saw bullets strike the asphalt on the other side of the road, sending up sand. My father got a running start and jumped for the top of the fence, put a foot on the crossbar, and nimbly hoisted himself up.

When my blocked view cleared, I saw two soldiers standing down the road. Mercenaries! They noticed us and came running. The guns thundered and bullets thudded into the asphalt.

'Hurry! They're right there!'

'Don't wait for me! Everybody run! Get away!'

With his words as the trigger, everyone set off sprinting at once. When I looked back, my father was following us.

We raced into the huge abandoned building. Machines that had been left behind slumbered silently in the gloomy gymnasium-like space. We ran on, threading our way between them.

At the other end was a steel door. It was open enough for one person at a time to squeeze by. We slipped through in single file.

Ahead we saw a small concrete building.

'Is this it?' Mr Akai asked my father who had caught up with us.

My father scanned the area and then turned back to the little building. 'I think so. It seems most likely.'

Mr Akai put his hand on the door. He turned the knob and pulled. It wasn't locked. Peering inside, he said, 'Stairs. They lead to the basement. This must be the entrance to the underground facilities.'

'Can you see anything?'

'I don't really know what it is, but… something's glowing.'

'Let's just go look. There's no time.'

Mr Akai nodded and ran down the stairs. My father went down after him. From right below, Mr Akai raised his voice. 'This must be the place! I see a world of white beyond the door!'

'Everyone come on down!' my father shouted. 'Hurry! We're going through the gate! We made it!'

17

The basement wall opened up into a white tunnel. Pale, slightly blueish light illuminated the inside here and there, though I didn't see a light source anywhere. Maybe the walls themselves were glowing. The brightness changed slowly as if the light was breathing.

The tunnel seemed to be about 30 metres in diameter. It curved almost imperceptibly to the left. A fog hung in the area. After we walked for a little while, we came upon a narrower tunnel branching diagonally off to the right. We wavered for a little while, but decided to go down that one. It was better to take side paths if we wanted to lose anyone chasing us. Fifteen minutes later, we reached another branch. We chose the narrower one there, too.

After two hours of consistently choosing the narrower path at each branch, the diameter of the tunnel was about a fifth of what it had been. The curve was sharper, too – a curvature radius of 100 metres or so.

There were side paths along the way, but we chose to ignore them. They were so narrow they seemed liable to make us anxious in a claustrophobic way.

In addition to those, there were sometimes openings in the tunnels that connected to oblate spaces. We decided to rest inside one.

We lay down like spokes of a wheel in the 20-metre diameter room. The walls were the same snow-white of the tunnel, and everything was so curved that it gave the place a strange atmosphere. It felt as if we were floating in a cloud, and the fog only heightened that impression.

What the walls were made of was a mystery. They looked smooth like tile, but when you touched them they were soft. Maybe they were made of some type of porous material.

Takuya was close to having an attack after running so much. I hugged him close and rubbed his back. His little heart was beating at a furious pace.

My brother had been frail ever since he was small and would get these attacks where it was hard to breathe. There was no miracle drug for it, so me rubbing his back seemed to be the only way to treat it. Strangely, that seemed to help the most.

These days most children had some issue or another. The world was completely polluted – the water, the air and the land. I think humans are amazing. We took such a beautiful planet of water and, in a matter of a hundred years, we turned it into a grimy mud ball.

The pollution got into our bodies. It affected each person differently, but I had the feeling our race was nearing its limit. The trend of infertility spreading across every continent was drawing an ominous curve that predicted our future.

I put my hand behind my brother's heart and rubbed it slowly up and down in time with my breath. I drew a gentle arc on his little back to synchronise our pulses.

'You're okay. You can breathe now, right?'

Takuya nodded in silence.

After a little while longer, his pulse settled down. A little colour had returned to his sheet-white face. He was fine.

Yusuke said this power of mine was another sign of the end-of-times.

'It's a special power motherhood requires. When you wish hard for someone to live, the energy sleeping inside you activates. You're like a real-life Wonder Woman, Aimi!'

Really? I wasn't so sure... but that would be brilliant if it were true. I mean, I had wished for that forever. The poison that greedy adults had thoughtlessly leaked was making children suffer like this. I had to stop it.

I wished for more power. '*How great would it be if I could heal all the children in this world...?*'

My father and the other adults had been talking for a while. We had to decide what to do next. The soldiers following us were a concern, but the bigger problem was how to get ahold of some food and water. We had only brought a tiny amount with us. At the rate we were going, we'd run out in just three days.

'What is this place?' said Mr Akai, a bit irritated. 'Isn't this our destination? Isn't this the white shelter of peace and calm?'

'Honestly, I have no idea.' My father shook his head. 'If this is where we were supposed to go, we should meet the people who went through the gate ahead of us. There are other refugees who received the signals. But we haven't seen anyone at all…'

'In other words,' said Mr Akai, 'there's another world outside this one, and everyone went there? Are you saying this is just a big entrance hall?'

'I think it's highly likely that's the case. Or everyone else is in an area we haven't seen yet. Maybe our true destination is an area somewhere in here set up with survival supplies…'

'So then we need to find that. Or a door to the outside.'

'Yes, that's what we'll have to do.'

'The problem is that we have no idea which way to go,' my mother suddenly chimed in.

The men both looked up at her, startled. Before the conflict started, my mother had been a high school biology teacher. Her voice had a strange persuasiveness to it.

'Judging from the curvature of the first tunnel, this maze is several kilometres in diameter,' she continued. 'If we walk around randomly, we really will end up wandering forever. We need to find some sort of sign.'

'When we came through the gate we were so desperate to escape the soldiers chasing us. Maybe we missed something?'

'So do you want to try going back, for starters?'

'But the soldiers…'

'Their objective was to find the gate and the white world. They may have followed us, but they're not interested in us anymore.'

'I hope you're right…'

So we agreed that our plan was to go back to where we had come from. That said, we were really tired, so we decided to rest where we were first. Takuya was already snoozing beside me. I rested my head on my pack and closed my eyes. A black veil came softly down, and in the next moment I had already fallen asleep.

During that brief moment of sleep, I had a dream. A memory of when we were happy.

On a rooftop at night, I was talking to Yusuke with my head on his shoulder. 'I heard that a long time ago, when we were at war with another country, our country banned love songs… Love is always an eyesore

22

to them. I'm sure my father's book was banned for the same kind of reason.'

'The power of love frightens them. Because love is tolerant. It operates on another level from narrow-minded heroism. They're scared that the people will realise that. A world filled with hateful words is their ideal, right? *Punish Thine Enemies.* That's why the weaponised-word mongers are out there evangelising.'

'Weaponised-word mongers?'

'Hateful words are just like bullets. The media has been at the beck and call of The Complex for ages now. The more hate speech spreads, the more hate grows in people's hearts. It's like a zombie virus. Anyone who comes into contact with it gets their blood flooded with aggressive factors.'

'Aggressive factors?'

'Like testosterone. Makes people aggressive. The world is full of such stories.'

'I can't handle those stories,' I said, shaking my head. 'I just can't stomach them. Everyone in my family is the same way. Why does everyone want to see stories about people hating each other and fighting? …Is it weird to think that way?'

'I think it's fine…' he said quietly, 'even if it is weird.'

'Really?'

'Yeah,' he nodded. 'And I'm the same way. If not wanting to see people hating each other is weird, then I want to stay weird forever. We were born without the hate function. That's why we're refugees. We don't get furious, we get frightened. We don't hate, we feel sad. To peaceful creatures like us, their culture is too violent – reality, TV dramas, videogames, all of it. They want everyone to accept that culture as normal, but we can't do it…'

—I heard someone breathing in my ear. Slowing exhaling, then inhaling… *'Who is it? Yusuke?'* I opened my eyes and quietly turned to look.

There was no one there.

I felt all the hairs on my body stand up. I held my breath and strained my ears. I could hear something from beyond the wall directly above my head. A receding presence. Not like footsteps – the sound was like something being dragged. No, I couldn't be sure. Maybe it was just my imagination.

I put my ear to the wall. I couldn't hear anything anymore…

When my mother saw me, she asked, 'What's wrong?'

'Nothing.' I shook my head. I didn't want to say too much and scare Takuya and Aoi. 'I think I was just having a dream…'

After about a three-hour break, we set off again. We proceeded cautiously, listening out for what might be up ahead. It wasn't very hard to go back the way we came. We had repeatedly chosen routes diagonal to the one we were on, so this time we just had to follow them back in reverse.

After about 40 minutes, we hit a dead end.

'What could this mean?'

'Did we take a wrong turn?'

'No,' I said. 'Look.' I pointed at our feet. There were dark marks on the bottom of the curved white surface. 'These are our footprints. I think it's grease from the factory floor.'

'So then…' My father put a hand to the white wall blocking the way we had come. 'That would mean this appeared after we passed through…?'

'It's bizarre, but that must be it.'

'What should we do?' Mr Akai asked anxiously. 'Our path is completely blocked…'

'Let's go back,' my mother said. 'A little while ago we passed a side path, didn't we? Maybe we can get back to the main tunnel from a different route if we go that way.'

The side path was one and a half metres in diameter at most – the adults couldn't walk down it without stooping. '*If we go in and the entrance gets blocked by another wall...*' Just the thought of it made my chest tight, and a cold sweat seeped out of my palms.

'Are you okay?' I asked Takuya. My brother is sensitive to people's unease and anxiety. Maybe that's another one of those end-of-times developments.

'Yeah,' he answered. I reminded myself that I mustn't look tense in front of him.

The corridors up until now had all curved in one direction, but this narrow tunnel twisted and turned so much that we couldn't see up ahead. It made everyone even more nervous. I was keeping my eyes fixed on my father's back, doing my best not to hyperventilate as I walked silently on, and after a bit I heard Mr Akai's voice from the front of the group. 'It's the exit! This corridor is much bigger!'

We emerged into a tunnel like before, with a slight curve. The diameter was about ten metres. It almost felt like we'd returned to the spot we'd entered, so I put a pen mark on the wall.

'Which way should we go?' Mr Akai asked.

My mother replied, 'This way, I think. This way must lead to the main tunnel.'

We set off walking again. The rules were the same. When we reached a branch, we went for the obtuse angle. If we did that, we assumed we would carry on to an even wider tunnel. After walking like that for two hours, we came out into a tunnel that seemed like the original corridor.

'I think this is probably the corridor we first entered,' my father said, looking up at the top of the tunnel, which must have been 30 metres high. 'This sure is a huge structure though. The Builders are incredibly skillful.'

We used the obtuse angle method again and proceeded toward the entrance. We walked cautiously since it was possible there were still soldiers there. However…

'It's a dead end…' my father murmured.

We'd hardly gotten anywhere at all before we came upon a huge wall blocking our path. Taking a look, I said, 'The soldiers were here. This is definitely the tunnel we came into originally.'

The soldiers had left footprints. There were also cigarette butts and food wrappers littering the ground (as well as what looked like signs that nature had called someone).

'I wonder where they went,' Mr Akai said, scanning the area anxiously.

'At any rate,' my father said, 'let's look for some sort of clue.'

After about ten minutes, everyone had searched the walls and tunnel, but we didn't find a single thing that seemed like it could be a clue.

'We're totally stuck, huh?' My father rubbed his stubbly chin. 'And we have no way to get back to the other world. All we have to go by is our own intuition and powers of deduction. So what should we do?' My father looked over to me.

'I think...' I said, 'we should go deeper down the corridor.'

'Is that your special refugee power?'

'Yep. My custom instinct is telling me that.'

'Understood,' my father nodded. 'Let's follow that instinct.'

After advancing for a little while, we passed the branch where we had come out earlier. There was a pen mark there, so I recognised it immediately. We went past without stopping. Deeper.

Was there some airflow in the tunnel? For whatever reason, a wind-like noise was coming from the end of the corridor. It was chilling because it sounded like the howl of a beast. The fog was as thick as ever, and sluggishly drifted in gentle swirls.

There were branches every few hundred metres. Mr Akai tried going into a number of the tunnels, but he said they were all the same. Who knows how many he had entered when he came out of one carrying a sturdy black leather boot.

'This was on the ground in a spherical room just a little way inside the tunnel.'

'That's a military boot, right?'

'Seems that way. Maybe it belongs to one of the people who were chasing us?'

'Maybe… We can't be sure.'

'It's just like an insectivorous snare…' my mother murmured.

'Huh? What?'

She shook her head that it was nothing. 'Never mind…' She looked a little pale.

That day our exploration ended after three hours of walking down the large corridor. A little way past the spot where we had gone down one of those side paths there was a spherical room, so we decided to rest there.

'What a huge space. I have no idea where we're heading…' Mr Akai said, rubbing his calves. 'We must have walked more than ten kilometres but…'

'Yeah, since our GPS and compasses don't work here, we have no idea what direction we're even going…'

'Is this really the shelter?' Mr Akai continued. 'If we don't find food or water soon, we'll—' Mrs Akai interrupted with a poke in her husband's side. She gestured at Aoi with a look. Aoi seemed frightened by all the uneasiness, as if she was about to start crying. Mr Akai cleared his throat softly and said nothing else.

'Mum, I need to pee,' said Aoi.

'Okay, let's go,' her mother answered.

The two of them disappeared into the corridor. I took a hard, dry hunk of bread out of my pack and crammed it into my mouth. I sipped a little water from a plastic bottle. Less than half remained. Mr Akai was right. If we didn't find food and water soon, we were going to be immobilised by starvation and thirst...

Suddenly we heard a little scream. It was Aoi's voice. I jumped to my feet and rushed out into the corridor. All the remaining adults followed. The pair was less than ten metres away. Aoi was pulling her jeans up in a panic.

'What happened?'

'There was someone there!' said Aoi. 'A white shadow was coming over here through the fog...'

'A shadow?'

'Yeah. It looked like a person made of fog. When I screamed, it disappeared.'

I looked at her mother, Yuko. She shook her head. 'I didn't notice anything. I was looking the other way.'

'I'm telling the truth!' said Aoi on the brink of tears. 'There was really someone there!'

I walked in the direction she pointed. The fog was thick, so I couldn't see very far. Suddenly, I seemed to smell something. A lingering scent brushed the tip of my nose. A fresh green odour so faint I could hardly tell if it was really there or not…

And I heard something, too. Not from across the corridor, but below – beneath the ground I was standing on, I heard someone breathing… But then it was gone.

'Aimi, be careful.' I heard my father's voice at my back.

'Don't worry. I won't go far.'

My toe hit something – *dink*. I bent down to pick it up. It was a big pine cone. I went back to show it to everyone.

'I found this on the ground.'

'A pine cone, huh?' my mother said. 'But how did that get there?'

'Maybe that shadow person left it?'

'Ugh, don't frighten us like that.'

'Maybe another refugee dropped it,' my father said. 'They might have left it as a marker.'

'Like the breadcrumbs in 'Hansel and Gretel'?'

'Yes, like that.'

But it was clear that no one believed that. Everyone was staring at the pine cone with fear in their eyes.

'There's something here… I sense some kind of presence…'

It was true.

'There's something here…'

Before sleeping, I asked my mother, 'What's an insectivorous snare?'

She hesitated for a moment but then lowered her voice and said, 'It's the organ a carnivorous plant uses to catch bugs.'

'Huh? So you mean this room is…?'

'We're fine. There aren't any digestive juices or anything here, right? I just thought of it suddenly and it slipped out, that's all.'

'But…'

'We're really okay, so don't worry. Maybe The Builders are protecting us…'

I nodded. 'I somehow have that feeling, too…'

'Go to sleep now.' My mother kissed my hair. 'I'm sure it'll be another long day tomorrow…'

Our secret place was an abandoned old-fashioned bus. We would sit next to each other on the holey seats seeking a moment's respite in the dusty-smelling darkness.

'I'm scared,' Yusuke whispered into my ear one time. 'You seem like such a fragile, fleeting presence, Aimi. Is this a side effect of love?'

'It'll be all right,' I told him. 'I'm strong. When Sae read my palm, she said I would live to be 100.'

He laughed quietly. 'I hope so… Then we can rain a hundred years of love on this earth. We'll live just as long as Methuselah – that'll show them. We'll take this planet, filthy with hatred and loathing, and clean it up to make a paradise for monkeys who want to love.'

'Sounds wonderful.'

'Right?'

Yusuke kissed me. I opened my lips just a little to receive him. The hairs on my back slowly rose. When I shivered he asked, 'Are you cold?'

I shook my head. 'No, I'm happy.'

'Aimi...' I thought I heard Yusuke calling me and jumped up. But he wasn't there. The adults had been awake for a while and were getting ready to go.

'Did you sleep well?' my mother asked.

'Yeah... I feel like I must have had a really good dream...'

We walked that whole day, too. Takuya and Aoi were getting exhausted. We were making sure they got food and water before anyone else, but even so, I had the feeling they were nearing their limits.

Whether we were walking or resting, all my father and Mr Akai talked about was, *'How did the world end up like this?'* Mr Akai is ten years younger than my father, so it was just like a teacher and a student.

'...So the anti-government army was doomed from the start?'

'Yes, that's what I think. Fighting military might with military might is senseless. Blood-spattered ideals are the seeds of violence. Fighting using our opponents' rules is a mistake in the first place. I mean, an army that specialises in military prowess has been refining their fighting techniques for thousands of years.'

'That's true...'

'I saw a statistic showing that in the past 100 years, nonviolent resistance has been twice as likely to succeed than violent resistance. That number says it all.'

'So then why do so many people still call for violent methods?'

'They underestimate the power of women. Actually, many women are involved in nonviolent movements. Men stuck in the patriarchal mindset can't seem to stand it... They think institutional, patriarchal justice is the only justice – because the world is full of such stories. And then even innocent young girls take up guns and swords to kill the enemy. Those men probably never thought about the fact that Florence Nightingale was a woman... or the significance of her work and her tolerance. On a battlefield where men were madly killing each other, at least the women managed to stay sane and tried to save lives without distinguishing between friend or foe...'

The day ended after another ten kilometres or so of exploration. We didn't discover anything, and the large corridor seemed to stretch on endlessly. The adults were tense and scared. The Akai family seemed to doubt whether we could go any further.

I was sitting on the curved white floor reading the letter Yusuke left me when Aoi asked, 'What are you reading?'

'A letter from Yusuke.'

'Is Yusuke your fiancé, Aimi?'

'Yes. Well, that's what we called each other.'

'What does it say?'

'He says he's sorry for leaving me alone and disappearing… His father was the leader of an anti-government organisation. They were known as a moderate faction and hoped for a nonviolent end to the conflict. But the public security forces were after him, so he took his whole family and fled.'

'Where did they go?'

'In the letter Yusuke said the plan was to "go through the gate". He said that it wasn't just to escape danger, but that there was something they needed to do, and that's why they were going.'

'Is that why you're going, too?'

I nodded. 'I can't help but feel like Yusuke is calling me…'

Someone was speaking in a low voice. It woke me up, so I looked around to see where it was coming from.

My backpack!

I stuck my hand inside and pulled out my clock radio. It had started picking something up on its own. Beyond the shower of static, a muffled voice was talking.

I recognised the voice. It belonged to a friend and classmate of mine I got along with well – Aki. She was raped and killed by an anti-government guerilla.

But she was trying to tell me something. She was reciting a ten-digit number over and over. I wrote it on my arm.

The last time I'd received a *broadcast* from her, it was the longitude and latitude of the open gate. Apparently, that's how people learn where to go. The coordinates come through radios or mobile phones; sometimes they even show up on broken TVs.

The notifications only go to devices belonging to refugees, never to the soldiers. When the gate opens, refugees within roughly a 50-kilometre radius get the message. But not all of them. Only certain people. I have no idea what the selection criteria are, but apparently lots of refugees have passed through the gate in that way.

And now… Aki had given me new numbers. '*Is this some kind of clue?*'

The noise woke my mother up, and she looked at the numbers written on my arm.

'I think… that's the golden ratio.'

'The golden ratio…?'

'Yes, I'm pretty sure. It often appears in nature. Tree branches exhibit the Fibonacci sequence, but the way these numbers get progressively closer together – it must be an approximation of the golden ratio. The spirals you find in the natural world are the same way.'

Then it came to me in a flash. 'The pine cone!'

'Yes! That's a spiral. The scales grow around an axis in a corkscrew pattern.'

'So this is what The Builders were trying to tell us.'

'About spirals?'

'Yes, the spirals. This huge corridor isn't just curving, it's tracing a spiral. I'm sure our destination is at the centre. The refugee radar was right!'

That guess changed into conviction as we advanced through the tunnel. The curvature radius got tighter and tighter. The tunnel diameter got smaller along with it – we were down to about a third of the original size. I couldn't sense any change in the slope. Apparently this shape is called a logarithmic spiral. That's what my mother told me.

'Come to think of it, all the branches were spiraling, too, weren't they?' she said. 'This world is full of self-similarity – logarithmic spirals are just one example.'

'Self-similarity?'

'Yes, you see it all the time in plant life, in the shapes of branches, leaves, flower buds…'

Suddenly, an explosion thundered behind us. Everyone stopped in their tracks and turned around.

'What was that?!' my father shouted.

'Shh!' Mr Akai said, putting a finger to his lips. 'I can hear something…'

As soon as he said that, everyone fell silent. We held our breath and listened. Someone was yelling far away. It was a man's voice.

'…*Up ahead, right?*'

'…*Yes, no doubt about it…*'

'…*Okay, we're continuing on. Private, clear the debris to secure us a path…*'

'It's government troops!' Mr Akai hissed.

'This is bad. We have to hurry!' my father said.

'Did they follow us?'

'Hmm, not sure. They do have brains, though, same as us. It's possible they came on their own, too, though.'

We broke into a jog and hurried on. My father carried Takuya on his back. I clutched the backpack he handed me to my chest.

After a little while, we suddenly came to an open area. This oblate space had a conical tower at its centre, maybe about 20 metres tall. The point disappeared into a hole in the ceiling.

'We have to climb! It must lead to the exit!'

The tower had a slope like a spiral staircase. There were no handrails or anything. One behind the other, we started going up. With every loop around, the bottom of the space grew further away. Now we had to battle acrophobia.

We had less than a third of the way to go, when soldiers suddenly poured into the hall. Had they noticed us? Gunshots rang out immediately. But we couldn't stop. We mustered the last of our energy and raced up the rest of the slope.

The hole at the top of the room was about five metres deep. Past that, we came out abruptly into a dark space. No matter how hard I strained my eyes, I couldn't see a thing. '*Is it some sort of enormous culvert?*' An instinctive fear of the dark welled up inside me. We moved from a white corkscrew world to a world of black darkness...

Once everyone made it to the top, the hole we had just come through began to shrink with a noise like popping bubbles. It was closing before our eyes. As if someone were dimming the lights, the area grew darker and darker.

'Someone really is watching over us...' my mother whispered.

The moment the hole was plugged, a soldier thrust his arm up with a roar, but it vanished almost instantly as if the ground had swallowed it up. All that remained was darkness and silence.

Eventually my eyes adjusted, and I could get at least a dim idea of our situation.

This was clearly the outside world. We weren't inside a giant structure or a culvert. It was an unfamiliar wasteland, and the only things around us were shrubs twisting in the wind. Even when I looked toward the sky, I couldn't see any stars. The earth occasionally rumbled below, almost as if there was an underground railway operating within.

'Where *are* we…?' Mr Akai murmured as he looked up at the sky.

'It seems like somewhere up north.'

'If the stars were visible, I'd have a rough idea, but…' my father said looking up at the sky. 'Like this, I can't see a thing.'

'We shouldn't be more than a few kilometres away from where we went through the gate…'

When I looked at the time, it was still three in the afternoon. So why was it so dark…?

'Were we transported to some far-off land without realising it?' I asked, and my father shook his head.

'Who can say…? Anyhow, let's get going. We have to find water no matter what…'

The compass was working again, so we decided to head north. Our feet were heavy – because we had been convinced that if we just escaped that white world we would reach the real shelter.

Leaving the small, shrub-scattered wood, we came out on a bald, rugged wasteland. Now and then we saw a little grassy patch, but other than that there was no sign of life. In the end, after walking for about three hours, we decided to stop the search for the day.

We ate a simple dinner in the hollow we chose as our campsite. If we didn't replenish our food and water supplies soon, we really would have our last supper. Everyone was terribly anxious.

My brother was in rough shape. Takuya was small to begin with, so he didn't have reserves to burn, and was the first to reach the point of starvation. He said he was cold, so I wrapped the two of us up in a thermal sheet and held him.

'Sis,' he said.

'Hm? What?'

'Am I… going to die soon?'

For a second, I couldn't say a thing. *'Is that what he's thinking in that little head of his…?'*

'Don't worry,' I said. 'You won't die. We're going to survive. That's why we've fought to get this far.'

I held his little head to my chest. When I put my hand on his back to rub it, I could feel how much weight he had lost. For a second, I thought, '*If only my breasts would make milk…*' And '*Then he wouldn't have to be so hungry anymore…*'

Then… something extraordinarily weird happened. I had the feeling milk was filling my breasts, even though there was no way that could be true. Something warm was welling up deep in my chest and flowing into Takuya's body. Of course, that's only how I saw it in my head – it wasn't reality, just something I imagined, but… Even so, the feeling was strangely real and intense.

'Mm…' Takuya murmured softly. 'It's yummy…' He moved his mouth and his little pink tongue poked out.

'What…? Did you feel something?'

He didn't answer. Before I knew it, he had fallen asleep with a peaceful smile across his emaciated cheeks.

I tried touching my chest. It wasn't wet. Of course it wasn't. That couldn't have happened. But… then what *was* it? Just a hallucination? Or was it one of those things where everyone has the power within them and at the right moment it suddenly awakens? Do I have the ability to share this milk-like substance inside me, like a life-force, with starving people…?

'*Maybe something inside me is waking up…*' That was the thought I had.

After resting for five hours or so, we wearily rose and continued walking north. The sky was just as dark as before. We had reached the end of both our food and water supplies. If we didn't find something today, we'd all dry out and end up as mummies.

After walking for an hour, my father abruptly raised his voice in apprehension. 'Look.'

When I shifted my gaze to the direction he was pointing, I saw a small light in the distance.

'What's that? Government troops?'

'No, it's something else… It honestly looks like a torch. See how it's flickering? It's coming closer.'

'Heyyy!' a voice yelled. 'Is someone there?'

'We're refugees!' my father shouted back. 'Who are you?'

'I'm on patrol duty!' the voice said. 'I'm picking up newly arrived refugees.'

The man on patrol duty was tall and getting on in years. He had short grey hair and wore round glasses. He said his name was Tokuyama.

'I'm so glad you made it safely. You're all right now. You can relax.'

'You mean…' my father said. 'We're…?'

'Yes. You've finally reached the shelter. We have food and water. There are lots of refugees living here.'

We cheered. Everyone joyfully hugged each other. We were all sobbing.

'Thank you…' my father said through his tears. 'Thank you so much… We made it, everyone…'

Tokuyama told us the village where the refugees lived was two hours away. With him as our guide, we set off.

'Where we're heading is a strange place. It's sort of like the Land of Memory from *The Blue Bird*.'

'What was that story about, again? I don't really remember…' my father said, and Tokuyama grinned mischievously.

'You'll understand when we get there. It'll be a surprise.'

'Where does the food and water come from?' asked Mr Akai.

'We have enough to eat for the near future. After that, we'll have to be self-sufficient. We'll plough the fields, keep chickens, raise goats. The soil here is amazingly rich – anything we plant comes up quick and healthy. Or maybe the seeds we have are special somehow… We also have plenty of water. It's a marshy area. We have everything we need.'

'There are chickens and goats?'

'It's hard to believe, right? But there are. Some of the refugees are farmers, and they brought their livestock with them to the shelter. They're very important people – like children of Noah. Thanks to them, we're slowly starting to have eggs to eat and milk to drink.'

'The soldiers have never shown up here?' my father asked with concern.

Tokuyama shook his head no. 'The Builders' filtering system functions bizarrely well. Soldiers are completely excluded. I have no idea how it works, but we've never once seen any. It's peaceful here.'

Tokuyama said the refugees here lived similarly to Quakers. There were no precepts, and furthermore, there wasn't even an agreed-upon dogma. Every individual was absolutely free. Still, they all loved peace and were happy to live simple lives.

'It sounds like a hippy commune,' said Mr Akai. 'Freedom, peace, and love…'

'Well, when you recall that the hippies were the ones who really started making anti-war noise, maybe it's only natural that we're similar. Perhaps this is Haight-Ashbury minus the drugs. Their motto back then was "Back to nature", which is a fascinating point of similarity. We all love nature. The culture that is quietly taking root here could almost be called a basic sort of tree worship.'

'What's Haight-Ashbury?' I asked my father, and Mr Akai answered in his place.

'It's known as the birthplace of the hippies. It's in San Francisco.'

'You were saying something about drugs, though.'

'LSD,' my father said. 'At the time, hippies were using it to expand their consciousness.'

'When you think about it...' Mr Akai seemed to be pondering something; he stared at his feet. 'The LSD and meditation were both about awakening their minds, right?'

'Yes, that's what I've heard... In order to resist the system's misinformation – which included starting the movement against the war – they needed to reach a higher level of consciousness...'

'Actually,' Mr Akai said, holding his palms up in front of him. 'I think it actually fits right in with the "Back to nature" idea. Although I'm not sure how aware of that they were at the time...'

'What do you mean?' I asked, and Mr Akai smiled at me.

'Apparently there are forces in nature that awaken human consciousness. When we come into contact with them, they act like switches to activate genes that have been dormant.'

'Really?'

'Yeah, that's what they say. Due to urbanisation and industrialisation, we've been living apart from nature, right? Apparently that turns off these genes we're supposed to have, and they go into a type of sleep-mode.'

'Ugh, so you mean we're half-asleep?'

'Compared to ancient people. That's just what modernisation is. And it's not all due to being out of touch with nature. Less physical activity, disrupted circadian rhythm, junk food with low nutritional value – those are all side effects of modernisation. They all turn our genes off. An interesting point is that the treatment for depression involves the opposite of all those things. Exercise, light-therapy, diet... In other words, anti-modernisation and anti-urbanisation. Some people say these trends already existed back when we were first starting to farm. Humans are monkeys who are sad about how weak they've become.'

'I read a story similar to that,' my father said. 'Urbanisation and industrialisation breed cynicism and nihilism – in other words, another form of depression. Passive people with lowered brain activity surrender their lives to someone else without deciding a single thing for themselves. There are only two criteria for making decisions: Is it information that they've seen with high frequency? Is it information shared by someone influential? Then all they have to do is quietly obey. People in authority take advantage of that – using the media as their puppet.'

'The media?'

'Yes. They make clever use of the depressed and vulnerable population's instinctual desire to be part of a group. Hitler's right-hand man Goering said it, too. "That's easy," he said. "All you have to do is tell them they are being attacked and denounce the pacifists for lack of patriotism and exposing the country to danger. It works the same way in any country".'

'No way...'

'There's a statistic that shows that less than 20 per cent of people are so selfish they're always thinking about usurping others. That minority idolises anyone with authority; using each other and being used, those two groups manipulate the depressed masses and feed on the world. In that sense, the actual problem is the majority, these greyed-out people. They're the key to revitalising the world. They can isolate those in power – that is, starve them of human resources. Apoptosis – we need to cause The Complex to die from the inside out.'

'Is that really possible?'

'Yes, we need to build a global network to spread the skill of *waking up*. "Rather than being happy livestock, be miserable slaves!". That's where we have to start.'

When we reached the outskirts of the refugee village, there was a hint of light and some faint colour in the eastern sky. I was so used to the gloom that the orangey sunrise hurt my eyes.

Once I could get a look at our surroundings, I saw that this was completely different from the wasteland we'd been walking through. For starters, there were trees. The fresh leaves gleamed with life. I was very happy to see that. I must have missed green more than I realised.

After another ten minutes, Tokuyama, at the head of the group, suddenly stopped. He turned around to look at us.

'Do you see that over there?' He pointed at a hollow between two hills. 'In that valley, by the edge of the marsh.'

'Yeah,' my father said. 'There's a house. It…'

'Have you seen it somewhere before?'

'It looks a lot like our house…'

'I thought that might be the case. A few days ago, it was suddenly there.'

'What do you mean "it was there"?' my father asked.

'It's odd,' Tokuyama said. 'They just show up at some point. Without us realising. It usually happens when it's especially foggy, and often at night. It's not as if someone builds them, more as if they suddenly sprout out of the ground. That's the signal that new refugees are on their way.'

'But… why does it look exactly like our house?'

'It's not just the outside. The layout inside and the furniture are all perfectly replicated. We don't know why. Maybe it's a trivial exercise for The Builders.'

'So, is our house here, too?' asked Mr Akai.

'Yes. There are a few other houses that appeared around the same time, so it's probably amongst them. They're about a kilometre away. Shall I show you?' Tokuyama turned to my family and said, 'I'll stop by again tomorrow. Have a good rest today.'

I couldn't quite believe it. Our house, which had been totally demolished in an air raid, was standing there exactly as it used to look. On the wooden decking in the front garden were the bonsai trees my mother's father had carefully cultivated. My grandfather was a gardener.

'Even that black pine is here…'

It was a magnificent black pine bonsai said to be over 300 years old, my grandfather's favourite. He used to tell me, 'A tree this old has a soul, and if you listen closely enough, you can hear its voice.'

'Its voice?' I had asked.

'Yes, tree spirits sing. The rustling of their leaves, their elegant fragrance – truly the melody of the heavens.'

That grandfather was gone now. Shortly after the war ended, he was attacked by someone and died.

'So that's what Mr Tokuyama meant about the Land of Memory from *The Blue Bird*,' my mother said.

'What's the Land of Memory?'

'It's the name of the first country Mytyl and Tyltyl visit. They walk through a dense fog and, when they emerge into the light, they see a farmhouse. There they meet their dead grandparents and their siblings. It was a place where memories were kept, where you could encounter precious times from your past…'

The front door was open. We nervously went inside and took our shoes off before entering the hall. It smelled just like our old house. The way the floor creaked with every step was the same, too. When we opened the door at the end of the hallway, the dining room and kitchen were there, exactly as they had been.

'Look!' my mother shouted. 'The table and the sideboard are here!'

It was just as she said. The sideboard even had plates and cups in it.

'That's my cup!' Takuya chirped.

My mother opened the door and picked up the yellow elephant mug. 'It even has the little chip on the lip.'

When she handed it to Takuya, he cheerfully pretended to drink water. 'Yeah, this is what it was like. I remember!'

My father stood by the sink and turned on the tap. 'As I thought, no running water. This is just for decoration.'

'The lights, too,' my mother said. 'Do you remember this antique lamp? We splurged on it after your first book came out.'

'Oh yeah, that Italian chandelier you wanted for so long. It went well with this old house.'

'It's sort of strange,' my mother said. 'To think that we had such a time... We were so happy, and there was nothing to be afraid of...'

'Maybe that's what this house is here for,' my father said brushing a hand along the baby's breath-patterned wallpaper.

'What do you mean?'

My father got a faraway look in his eyes. '*Nostalgie*. During war a long time ago, rampant "nostalgia" amongst soldiers on the front was a huge issue. It spread among those men who were far from home, spending days with the threat of death constantly near, and psychiatrists at the time considered it an illness. Refugees are the same. We need healing. Maybe this is the best medicine...'

'Oh...'

'An everlasting hometown outside the flow of time...' my father murmured and rubbed the wallpaper. 'So we went on a big, long journey and finally returned home...'

Everything in my room was reproduced exactly, too. My bed, my desk, my white wardrobe, and the little dresser were all there. My favourite pink hairband was in the drawer. An old ring my mother had given me and my velvet choker.

I put the ring on my ring finger and lay down on my bed. I held my hand before my eyes and admired the little garnet in its setting. The pale light that came in through the window made it gleam red. It was so pretty... Before I knew it, I was crying. The memories of how innocent I had been came flooding back. I could never go back to those days. I had been so happy...

I let myself cry and soaked in the sentimental comfort of my reminiscence. The cleansing effect of the tears turned my pain into something else. Something sweet, and sad, and soft...

'Yusuke...' I whispered. 'I miss you... I miss you so much...'

'*Aimi...*'

I thought I heard Yusuke call me and jumped up. He wasn't there. At some point, the sun had gone down. I must have slept for an awfully long time. Someone was singing somewhere. '*What is that?*' I went downstairs.

There was no one in the living or dining rooms. *'Where did everybody go?'* Following the singing, I went into the garden. The sky was stained deep red. The singing grew louder. The melody was intensely familiar. It made my chest hurt.

I looked at the bonsai on the deck. 'Are you singing?'

But they didn't say anything. When I glanced at the water's edge, I saw a faintly glowing figure. *'Is that…?'*

'Yusuke…? Is that you?'

The figure wavered and glided over to the other side of the inlet, receding.

'Wait!' I raced across the yard after the shadow. Up ahead was a wooden pier, and I went for it with zero hesitation. My feet pounded over the wet boards.

'Wait, Yusuke! Don't go!'

When I was halfway down the pier, it suddenly gave way. Like a crumbling clod of sand, the wooden boards burst into crystals and dispersed. I fell backwards into the water.

Deep green seaweed came and wrapped me up like tentacles. Strangely, I wasn't afraid.

'Yusuke…'

As I was dragged to the dark water's bottom, my consciousness began to fade…

When I looked up, countless stars were twinkling in the night sky. I was on a small boat floating down a narrow waterway.

'Aimi,' someone said. A man was sitting near the rudder.

'Grandpa!' I yelled. My voice was oddly muffled and left an echo in my ears.

'Where am I? Is this a dream? Or the Land of Memory?' I asked. My grandfather didn't say anything.

He smiled in silence.

'Is this heaven? Maybe that's why you're here.'

'I wonder…' my grandfather said. 'Maybe it's all of those things. There's no name for it. At any rate, this is the place you were heading for. Everything happened according to The Builders' plan.'

'The Builders…? Who are they, anyway?'

'The people trying to save this planet from destruction. That's why they summoned all of you.'

'Summoned…? But isn't this a shelter?'

'No,' my grandfather said. 'No, this isn't a shelter.'

'What are you saying? We thought this was the final evacuation site. Isn't that why we fled and went through all that suffering? If it's not, then…'

'Oh, don't say it like that. The purpose might be different, but this world still functions as a safe haven doesn't it? It'll heal the refugees better than any other place you could evacuate to…'

'Yeah, that's true, but…'

'Then it's fine, isn't it? Everyone can just rest. We all had such a hard time getting here…'

A wind whipped by, bending the reeds hard. A pungent, green odour swept past my nose.

'Hey, Grandpa,' I said. 'You know what this place is really for, right?'

'Yes,' he nodded. 'I do…'

'What is it? Tell me.'

He looked at me with kind eyes.

'You're… one of the chosen children.'

'Chosen?'

'The Builders made this world in order to find and nurture you. It's for cultivating the people who will save the planet…'

'Save the planet…? Us?'

'Sure you will. You were summoned for a purpose.'

'But,' I whispered, almost to myself, 'why me…?'

'The refugees' special abilities… or end-of-times developments? You can call them whatever you like,' said my grandfather, 'but this planet needs those powers – the energy to heal and soothe the sickened earth. You're seen as particularly talented, and that includes latent power…'

'Latent…? But if I don't even know I have it, then how do The Builders know?'

'That's what the shelter is for. The same goes for the white corkscrew world. It's all a vast sieve. The Builders are always watching. They can see deep into your mind.'

'How…?'

'They have Observers. Tiny little organisms that study you.'

I shivered. 'That's terrifying. I had no idea that was happening… Where were they?'

'Everywhere,' he said. 'The white fog, the shadowy figures… all of that. The Observers are always there. And they don't only observe, they also draw out your latent abilities. With the rustling of leaves and their elegant fragrance…'

'That song…?'

'Exactly.' He nodded, satisfied that I understood. 'And listen,' he said, looking me in the eye, 'the scent of vegetation is brimming with deep, deep insight. Humans can finally learn what's right and what's wrong.'

'From the smell?'

'That's right,' he said. 'Once upon a time, far above heaven, was a world called the Fragrant Land, and there dwelled the merciful Buddha of Accumulated Fragrance. He guided the celestial beings not with words, but with smells. It's said that his followers were able to gain all manner of benefits simply by appreciating various scents.'

'Is that how we were awakened, too?'

'Yes… but you're just getting started. This isn't your true power. It needs refining. Just like the Buddha, right? He only reached true enlightenment sitting under the Bodhi tree.'

I gasped and looked at my grandfather. 'Is that where we're going? To my Bodhi tree…?'

'That's right.' He nodded. 'You have pretty good intuition, there.'

'No.' I shook my head. 'I don't know anything…' The only thing on my mind was how badly I wanted to see Yusuke… I got here without feeling any sense of mission… 'Can I still do it, do you think?'

'That's fine,' my grandfather reasoned kindly. 'Your power is to love. You hope for the person you love so intently to be at peace. Your sacred gift is a heart that fervently wishes that others live. You're a giver. You cuddle up to someone, heal them, and open their hearts… The children's powers seem to have something in common. One girl has a talent for predicting the future. Maybe a boy is exceptionally observant and persuasive… You're all children of one big family – the refugees. Siblings, each with your own idiosyncrasies. You're the descendants of a people who spent much of their lives on the run, hoping for peace and avoiding conflicts…

'But,' my grandfather continued, 'that's exactly why The Builders summoned you – because you're descendants of refugees. Those born without fists meant for punching… Those who are already hurting… Those are the people who will heal the world. Suffering women and children, the souls of the those who fell in war that still echo in the trees, the spirits that inhabit our horribly polluted natural world – these are the hands that will join together to restore the planet…'

'Okay…'

'Listen,' he said, lifting an index finger. 'In this world there is a single, neat, golden rule. It's a formal truth. And it is this…'– my grandfather jerked his chin up and loudly recited – *'No long-lived civilisation that leaves its footprints on a far-flung planet tolerates violence.'*

'Really?'

'Don't you understand? It's so obvious it requires no explanation. It's Prometheus's fire. Civilisation and military might are always correlated. The fate of a civilisation that can't overcome the instincts of belligerent discriminatory males is always – *always* – destruction. Power is fragile and perilous. If ever a civilisation is able to escape the curse of male oppression, those who inherit the planet will be descendants of refugees. The Builders knew that…'

I had no words. I felt I'd learned something terribly important.

This planet was entrusted to the weakest, the children… The voiceless will heal and inherit the planet. Refugees are the true successors to civilisation… or at least that's what The Builders think, and they've chosen us…

'Am I enough…?' I asked softly.

'Yes.' My grandfather nodded. 'It has to be you…'

The boat carried us soundlessly along. The night sky was still full of stars, unfamiliar constellations telling ancient tales in hushed tones. We passed beneath a few huge bridges. They seemed like remains left by prehistoric giants.

'What are those?'

'Who knows?' my grandfather said. 'Probably someone's memories…'

'Memories?'

'Weren't you all saying that? That this is the Land of Memories…? Only the hearts of weakened monkeys fall under materialism's spell. The world is much deeper than that. The beings who created these are living on beyond the bounds of time. There's a vision here woven of memories along with reality.'

'Okay, we're here,' my grandfather said. 'Your fiancé can't wait to see you.'

When I looked to the shore, the abandoned old-fashioned bus was there.

'Yusuke's *here*?'

'Yes… He is one of the chosen, too. But he's wounded and in pain. They were attacked on their way through the gate, and he was separated from his family. Though seriously injured, he still managed to make it here. Now's the time to put your powers to the test. Can you do it?'

I nodded silently.

'Good girl. That's my granddaughter.'

'Thank you, Grandpa. I'll do my best, so make sure you watch…'

'I'll always be watching over you. Now, go on.'

'Okay! See you!'

Yusuke was asleep. He was wrapped shoulder to chest with bandages dark red with seeping blood. I took off my jacket and cuddled so close to him there was no space between us. For some reason, I knew what I needed to do. That's why I took my clothes off. We needed to be as close to skin-to-skin as possible.

Doing this felt connected in some way to how female animals know how to give birth without being

61

taught. Instincts were guiding me. They lectured me: *If you want to heal him, here is what to do.* All I did was follow the instructions. I would bring him back. I didn't know where he was now, but my breast was far warmer and softer…

I pressed my lips softly to his. This was a kiss of awakening. I would do it a million times if it would wake him up. I would breath life back into his withered soul as if I were inflating a balloon.

'Hey, Yusuke… You saved my life so many times. So now it's my turn. Just wait. We'll be together again soon…'

'If I wish from the bottom of my heart, I'm sure I can do it. No matter how many times I get knocked down, I can stand up again, hold the ones I love and keep a gentle watch over them, protecting their lives – because that's the ultimate power of us refugees.'

Aimi, Aimi… I woke up to a voice calling me.

When I opened my eyes, someone's face was right at the tip of my nose, so close it felt as if our foreheads might stick together. I looked up absentmindedly with an unfocused gaze.

'Aimi, are you awake?' A familiar voice…

'Yusuke…? Is it you?' I asked quietly, my voice shaking.

'Yes!' he said. 'At last we're together.'

'Phew!' I hugged him without thinking. 'You're better!'

'Yeah, thanks to you. I'm so much better now.'

He took my hand and led me out of the bus. We were deep in a forest. Looking up, I saw an unbelievably tall tree towering magnificently next to us.

'What a huge tree…' I murmured without really meaning to. 'So this is our Bodhi tree…'

'Hm?' said Yusuke. 'What do you mean?'

'Never mind', I shook my head. 'I feel like I had a super long dream…'

'Me, too. But we learned something important during it.'

He was right. I knew both how much power I had gained and what I needed to do with it.

We were 'The Entrusted Children.' And it wasn't only this place. There were locations all over the planet where children like us were awakening to their powers.

'Our hearts are all connected,' Yusuke said. 'No matter what obstacles they put in in our way, they'll never be able to divide us…'

'Yeah, you're right…'

The repulsive force of hate would try to tear us apart, but the hearts of awakened children are connected. Love is magnetic, so if we spread that power around the world…

'This is the coward's story,' said Yusuke said with a smile. 'Up till now, we've been relegated to the wings of the stage – because the world is overflowing with stories of heroes. But that's not what this planet wanted. That's a fantastic thing. The weaklings, and the crybabies, and the children who just want to love can be the heroes here. We're the Crybaby Earth Defense Force.'

'You really are so odd, Yusuke.'

'Hmm, you think so?'

I nodded. 'That's why I love you.'

Above our heads, the huge ancient tree spread its arms wide, and its green canopy waved in the wind.

The Builders had always been here like this. They were always nearby, living alongside us. They watched over us, guided us, helped us to notice things and loved us.

They'd been alive far longer than human beings. Their own consciousness had sprouted, and they deepened their intellects over a long, long period of time. Then they created a world far more rich and vast than we could ever have imagined. But the humans, blinded by greed, were about to ruin that world of abundance.

The Builders weren't fans of excessive intervention, so they didn't interact with us directly. Instead, they encouraged us to realise things for ourselves. And that's how we were entrusted, we proud children of refugees. We will heal and rejuvenate the injured world. If the destructive power of The Hero was the dream of patriarchal men, then our abilities are a magnified version of motherly love.

If we succeed the final gate will open, and we'll be welcomed as members of a far vaster world than we could have imagined. A kind world of abundance filled with love. No hatred, no war, and no children getting hurt by the selfish behaviour of adults…

The forest was singing. I hummed quietly along.

'Yeah… *When we return to our world, along with the fruit of this land, we should bring this song with us… We'll help the flower of life to bloom once more on this dead, emaciated planet.'*

Maybe a single song *can* change the world…

'In a dystopian world in which human suffering knows no bounds, Takuji Ichikawa gives us a glimmer of hope. One immediately thinks of the Gospel of Matthew: 'Blessed are the meek: for they shall inherit the earth.' With its moral undertones, this esoteric tale is apposite for our deeply divided society.'

Alex Pearl, author of *Sleeping with the Blackbirds*

'The power of his storytelling is due to the candour of the feelings expressed. As if, confusing reality, somewhat magically, is what makes literature compelling giving it the power to delight and please.'

Le Monde

'I felt it in my heart, and it shook my soul.'

Kiyoshi Kodama, actor and former presenter of a popular Japanese television book review programme, commenting on *Be With You*

'Reading this sent me into a trance. I discovered what love really is from this book.'

Ryoko Hirosue, Japanese actress best known outside Japan for her roles in *Departures* **and** *Wasabi*, **commenting on** *Love's Photographs*

Red Circle Minis

Original, Short and Compelling Reads

Red Circle Minis is a series of short captivating books by Japan's finest contemporary writers that brings the narratives and voices of Japan together as never before. Each book is a first edition written specifically for the series and is being published in English first.

The book covers in the series draw on traditional Japanese motifs and colours found in Japanese building, paper, garden and textile design. Everything, in fact, that is beautiful and refined, from kimonos to zen gardens and everything in between. The mark included on the covers incorporates the Japanese character *mame* meaning 'bean', a word that has many uses and connotations including all things miniature and adorable. The colour used on this cover is known as *fuji-iro*.

 Red Circle

Showcasing Japan's Best Creative Writing

Red Circle Authors Limited is a specialist publishing company that publishes the works of a carefully selected and curated group of leading contemporary Japanese authors.

For more information on Red Circle, Japanese literature, and Red Circle authors, please visit:
www.redcircleauthors.com